Katie Woo

Tries Something New

by Fran Manushkin
illustrated by Tammie Lyon

capstone

Katie Woo is published by Picture Window Books
A Capstone Imprint
1710 Roe Crest Drive
North Mankato, MN 56003
www.capstoneyoungreaders.com

Text © 2015 Fran Manushkin
Illustrations © 2015 Picture Window Books

Library of Congress Cataloging-in-Publication Data
Manushkin, Fran.
 Katie Woo tries something new / by Fran Manushkin; illustrated by Tammie Lyon.
    pages cm. — (Katie Woo)
  ISBN 978-1-4795-6182-7 (pbk.)
1. Woo, Katie (Fictitious character)—Juvenile fiction. 2. Chinese Americans—Juvenile
fiction. 3. Mother's Day—Juvenile fiction. 4. Helping behavior—Juvenile fiction.
5. Scouts (Youth organization members)—Juvenile fiction. 6. Hiking—Juvenile fiction.
[1. Chinese Americans—Fiction. 2. Mother's Day—Fiction. 3. Helpfulness—Fiction.
4. Scouts (Youth organization members)—Fiction. 5. Hiking—Fiction.] I. Lyon,
Tammie, illustrator. II. Title. III. Series: Manushkin, Fran. Katie Woo.
  PZ7.M3195Kbl 2015
  813.54—dc23
  [E]   2014042073

Photo Credits:
Greg Holch, pg. 96; Tammie Lyon, pg. 96
Designer: Kristi Carlson

Printed in United States of America, in North Mankato, Minnesota.
112016   010118R

Table of Contents

Cartwheel Katie 4

Katie's Noisy Music...................................26

Katie Woo, Super Scout 48

Katie's Happy Mother's Day.......................70

Cartwheel Katie

Katie and JoJo were watching
TV. Girls were doing cartwheels and
jumping on trampolines.

"Those girls are cool," said JoJo.

"For sure!" said Katie.

Her mom asked, "Would you like
to take a gymnastics class?"

"Yes!" yelled Katie. "Then I can be
a TV star."

"That may take a while," said her
mom. "But you'll still have fun."

Katie and JoJo went to class together.

"Welcome," said Miss Nimble. "Let's stretch first."

"I'm great at stretching," bragged Katie.

"You look like my cat," said JoJo.

"Now let's do somersaults," said
Miss Nimble.

"I can do those!" Katie bragged.
But she wiggled this way and wobbled
that way.

"This isn't so easy," said Katie.

Katie wanted to do perfect somersaults.

She practiced on the grass with Pedro. But his puppy did them better than she did.

It got worse the next day! The class started the balance beam.

"That looks easy," said Katie.

Oops! She kept falling down. "Not so easy," she groaned.

That night, Katie told her mom, "It's hard when it's not easy."

"That's all right," said her mom. "You are learning."

"I know," Katie sighed. "But I want to learn faster."

At the next class, Miss Nimble said, "We are a team. We work together and help each other."

"I need a lot of help," said Katie.

JoJo showed Katie how to do better somersaults. Katie tried again and again.

"Yay!" Katie cheered. "I'm not sideways anymore. I am upside down."

At the next class, Miss Nimble said, "Today we will begin cartwheels. They are tricky but lots of fun."

Mattie did great cartwheels.

But Katie fell to the right. Then she fell to the left.

"I don't like cartwheels," she decided. "They are silly."

"Don't give up," said Mattie.

"I'm not giving up," said Katie. But she was.

After class, Katie watched her mom playing tennis.

Sometimes she hit the ball. Sometimes she missed.

Katie asked her, "Don't you feel sad when you miss?"

"A little," said her mom. "But I keep getting better. I am proud of me."

At the next class, Katie watched JoJo do cartwheels.

Sometimes she did them. Sometimes she fell.

But she kept trying.

Katie said, "Maybe I'll try again.
I'll pretend I am the Little Engine that
Could."

Katie said, "I think I can! I think
I can!"

But she couldn't.

"Don't give up," said JoJo.

Katie tried a second cartwheel and a third. She kept falling.

"Try one more," said Mattie.

Katie tried again. She did it!

"I did it!" Katie yelled. "I did it. I
am proud of me."

"Yay!" said Miss Nimble.

"Now we will start the trampoline," said Miss Nimble. "Who wants to try?"

Hmm, thought Katie. *That looks tricky.*

"I'll try it!" decided Katie.

She was first in line.

Katie's Noisy Music

Katie's father was playing the piano. Katie loved the sounds he made.

She told her dad, "Your music makes me happy."

"You can make music too," said Katie's dad. "I can teach you to play the piano."

Katie played a few notes. They made a nice *plinking* sound.

"Hmm," said Katie, "I like the piano. But I'd like to play something of my own."

"I'll ask JoJo what to play," said Katie.

As she walked to JoJo's house, Katie ran a stick along a fence. She liked the *clickity-clackity* sound.

Katie asked JoJo, "What do you like to play?"

"I love my guitar," said JoJo.

She played "This Land Is Your Land," and Katie sang along.

"I can teach you to play the guitar," offered JoJo.

"That would be fun," said Katie. "But I'd like to play something of my own."

The next night, Katie and her
parents went to a school concert.

"I'd like to be on that stage," said
Katie. "I love the sound of clapping!"

After the concert, Pedro let Katie try his violin.

"Yikes!" she yelled. "My ears hurt."

"It takes a while to learn it," said Pedro.

"No, thanks!" said Katie.

Mattie let Katie try playing her
cello. It squawked and squealed.

"No way am I playing this," sighed
Katie. "Isn't there anything I can play?"

Katie was so unhappy, she kicked
a can all the way home. It made a fine
clinking and *clanking* sound.

Katie went to bed that night feeling sad. But when it began raining, the *pitter-patter* of the raindrops made her feel cozy. She fell asleep with a smile.

On Saturday, Barry took Katie to his accordion lesson at the music store.

"Let me try!" said Katie. "Wowza! It's nice and noisy but kind of heavy. Bye-bye, accordion!"

While she waited for Barry, Katie
tried playing a flute.

"It's very skinny," she said.

So she tried the tuba.

"It's too big!" sighed Katie.

"Nothing is right for me."

At dinner that night, Katie was so unhappy, she wasn't hungry. She just clicked her chopsticks together. *Click-clack-click.*

"Do that again," said Katie's mom.

Katie did: *click-clack-click.*

"I like that sound," said her mom.

Katie clicked some more.

"Guess what?" said her dad. "You are making music."

Katie banged a spoon on a pot.
"Is this music too?" she asked.

"Yes!" Her dad smiled.

"Yay!" said Katie, jumping up and
down. "I know what I want to play!"

"THE DRUMS!" they all said together.

"Absolutely!" added Katie's dad. "Katie and the drums were made for each other."

Katie began learning to play the drums. She made them go *click-clack, clank-clank,* and *boom-boom-BOOM!*

She made soft *tip-tip-tapping* sounds and *pitter-patter* raindrop sounds. All the sounds were music.

At the next school concert, Katie played the drums. As she took a bow, she said, "Music makes me happy!"

It made everyone else happy, too.

Katie Woo,
Super Scout

Katie and JoJo joined the Super
Scouts.

JoJo read the Scout Pledge: "We
promise to treat all scouts like sisters."

"That's cool!" said Katie. "I've
always wanted sisters."

Their leader, Miss Harris, said,
"Today, we are going for a hike in the
woods. Please pick a partner."

Janie, a girl Katie didn't know,
asked, "Will you be my partner?"

"Sure!" said Katie. "Hello, sister!"

"Our hike is a treasure hunt," said
Miss Harris.

"Yay!" yelled Katie. "I'm great at
those."

"I'm not," said Janie.

"Don't worry!" said Katie. "I'll help
you."

Janie read. "We need to find three things. The first one is a bug that fits on a penny."

"Ew, bugs!" said Katie.

"Yay, bugs!" cheered Janie.

As they walked, Janie called,
"Come here, bugs, bugs, bugs."

Katie yelled, "Go *away*, bugs, bugs,
bugs!"

Janie picked up a beetle and put it
on a penny. "Isn't he
cute?" she asked.

"Yech!" said
Katie. "Not to me."

"Yay!" said Janie. "The bug is our
first treasure."

"Now we need to find the second treasure," said Katie. "It's something blue. That sounds easy. I'm sure I'll find it first."

But Katie didn't. Janie did. "I found it!" she yelled. "It's these pretty blue periwinkles."

Katie felt bad. She said, "Why can't I find any treasures?"

Katie made a mean face at Janie and said, "I should have gone with JoJo. We always have fun."

Janie looked sad, but she didn't say anything.

Janie went off by herself. After a while, she began grabbing twigs and stacking them up.

"What are you doing?" asked Katie.

"I'm making a fairy house," said Janie. "Fairies live in the forest, but they have no place to sleep."

"What a nice thing to do!" said Katie. "Can I help you?"

"Sure!" agreed Janie.

Katie made a leafy roof, and
Janie lined the path to the house with
acorns.

"Here, fairies!" they called.

"I think fairies come at night," said Janie.

"Me too," agreed Katie. "It was fun making the house with you."

"I'm glad,"
said Janie. "Now
let's find the last
treasure."

Katie read,
"The last treasure must be as yellow
as the sun."

"I see it!" Katie pointed. "A pretty
birch leaf!"

"Good going!" yelled Janie.
"We did it!"

"Hey," Katie said, sniffing the air.
"I smell something sweet! Do you?"

"It's s'mores!" they yelled together.

"Let's hurry!" said Katie. "We don't
want to miss any!"

Katie and Janie held hands
and followed the sweet scent to the
campfire — and the other Super Scouts.

Katie told Janie, "I'm sorry I acted stinky. Will you still be my sister?"

"For sure!" Janie smiled. "Sometimes sisters might fight. But they are still sisters."

"Sisters, sisters, hurray!" chanted Katie.

The Super Scouts gathered around
the campfire. Katie said, "Janie, come
sit with me and JoJo."

JoJo made room for her.

"Let's have some more s'mores," yelled JoJo.

"Yes!" said Katie. "You can't have too many s'mores or sisters."

And it was true!

Katie's Happy Mother's Day

It was Saturday morning. Katie
was eating pancakes. But her mom
was not eating.

"What's wrong?" Katie asked her
mom.

"I don't feel well," she said.

"Maybe you should go back to bed," said Katie. "That's what I did when I had the flu."

"I think I will," said her mom.

"I will fluff up your pillow and
tuck you in," said Katie.

"This is cozy." Her mom smiled. "If
I sleep for a while, I'll feel better."

"Take my Teddy," offered Katie.
"When I hold Teddy, he helps me
sleep."

Katie's mom hugged Teddy tight.

Katie pulled down the shades, saying, "Bye-bye, sun. Mom needs to sleep now."

Katie's mom began to yawn. "I am feeling sleepy," she said.

"Good," said Katie. "I'll sing you a lullaby."

Katie sang, "Sleep, sleep, go to sleep. Dream of fluffy little sheep. You'll feel better when you wake — no more head or belly ache."

The lullaby worked! Katie's mom fell asleep. Katie tiptoed out of the room.

She called JoJo
and told her, "My
mom is sick."

"Oh, no!" said
JoJo. "Tomorrow
is Mother's Day. I
hope she's okay
by then."

When Katie's mom woke up, she looked a lot better.

"My headache is almost gone," she said. "You and Teddy and the nap really helped."

"Now you will have a happy
Mother's Day," said Katie.

But *Uh-oh!* thought Katie. *I don't
have a Mother's Day present for Mom.*

Katie's dad told Katie, "I got Mom
a necklace. It can be from both of us."
"Thanks," said Katie. "But I want
to give Mom something on my own."

Katie called Pedro and asked him what to do. He told Katie, "Why don't you make a card?"

"I'll paint a red one," said Katie. "Red is Mom's favorite color. But I want to give her a nice present too."

"I could give her flowers from our garden," said Katie. "She loves red roses. But none of them are blooming."

That night, Katie dreamed that
she painted the house red. Her mother
loved it!

But it was only a dream.

When Katie woke up, she felt sad. She didn't want to tell her mom, "I forgot to get you a gift."

But before Katie could say anthing, her mom said, "I have a surprise for you."

She gave Katie a pretty card. It said:

I'm the happiest mom that I can be!

Katie is the girl for me.

She is great in every way.

Every day is Mother's Day!

"I'm so happy!" said Katie.

"Me too!" said her mom, wiggling her toes.

"Aha!" said Katie. "Now I know what to give you — a pedicure!"

Katie painted her mother's toes a
bright, happy red.

"Wow!" said her mom. "My toes
and I thank you!"

Katie's grandma came over, and she got a pedicure too.

"Our daughters are the best," said Katie's mom and grandmother.

It was a very happy day!

Having Fun with Katie Woo!

Chinese Drum

In *Katie's Noisy Music*, Katie realizes she love the drums! Drums and other percussion instruments are used all over the world. You can make your own Chinese drum, perfect for playing at Chinese New Year or anytime.

Ingredients:

- Two small paper plates
- Popsicle stick
- Hot glue gun and glue
- Hole punch
- Two 7-inch ribbons
- Two beads

What you do:

1. Using the hot glue gun, glue the popsicle stick to the top of one of the paper plate edges to make the drum's handle.

2. Hot glue the two paper plates together.

3. Use the hole punch to punch a hole on each side of the drum.

4. String a ribbon through each hole and tie a knot to secure it. Then tie a bead on the other end of each ribbon.

Your drum is ready to play! Twist the handle back and forth to make the beads tap on the plates. You can also decorate your drum with drawings, Chinese characters, or pieces of colorful paper. Be creative and have fun!

Fairy House Fun

In *Katie Woo, Super Scout*, Katie and Janie make a fairy house using things they find in the woods. You can make a fairy house of your own while out hiking. Or follow these directions for a fun indoor craft.

What you need:

- an empty 20-oz soda bottle, washed and dried

- styrofoam cup (the opening should be wide enough to securely sit on top of the bottle)

- moss paper

- burlap fabric, cut into small strips

- glue

- yellow paper

- small sticks, leaves, seeds, stones, etc. for decorations

What you do:

1. Wrap and glue the moss paper around the soda bottle to cover the bottom 6-7 inches.

2. To make windows and a door, cut small squares or circles out of the yellow paper. Glue the shapes on the house. Then glue small twigs around the shape to make window and door frames.

3. To make the roof, glue burlap strips over the cup until the cup is covered, making sure that the burlap hangs over the rim slightly. Add leaves, seeds, or sticks to decorate the roof.

4. Place the cup upside down on top of the bottle. If you would like more decorations, add them. Else your house is ready for fairies!

About the Author

Fran Manushkin is the author of many popular picture books, including *Baby, Come Out!*; *Latkes and Applesauce: A Hanukkah Story*; *The Tushy Book*; *The Belly Book*; and *Big Girl Panties*. There is a real Katie Woo — she's Fran's great-niece — but she never gets in half the trouble of the Katie Woo in the books. Fran writes on her beloved Mac computer in New York City, without the help of her two naughty cats, Chaim and Goldy.

About the Illustrator

Tammie Lyon began her love for drawing at a young age while sitting at the kitchen table with her dad. She continued her love of art and eventually attended the Columbus College of Art and Design, where she earned a bachelors degree in fine art. After a brief career as a professional ballet dancer, she decided to devote herself full time to illustration. Today she lives with her husband, Lee, in Cincinnati, Ohio. Her dogs, Gus and Dudley, keep her company as she works in her studio.